Dog Trots Globe

To Paris & Provence

By Chula Wula D'Augue

As Barked to Sheron Long

Illustrations by Darius Detwiler

Photographs contributed by Robert and Sheron Long,
Erick Paraiso, and Meredith Mullins

O|C New Views into the World™

To good husbands and good dogs

OIC Books
OIC-Books.com
26385 Carmel Rancho Boulevard
Carmel, CA 93923

ISBN: 978-1-936951-00-0
11 12 13 14 15 16 / 10 9 8 7 6 5 4 3 2 1

Acknowledgments and Credits
OIC Books gratefully acknowledges the permission of copyright holders to reproduce works in this book. For Acknowledgments and Credits, see page 156.

Every attempt has been made to contact copyright holders to secure their permission for works used in this book and to secure model and property releases for images used. If any omissions have occurred, please contact the Publisher.

Printed in the United States of America.

Dog Trots Globe

To Paris & Provence

OIC Books
are enhanced with audio and video.
Visit **OIC-Books.com** and enjoy
more of this dog's eye view of France!

Contents

···· Foreword ····

A Sheltie Goes to France!

Chula, whose name means "pretty" in Spanish, set off for France with a smile.

An adventurous dog, she traveled by car from Carmel Valley, California, to San Francisco where she boarded an Air France flight to Paris. Then she took the TGV, or *Train à Grande Vitesse,* from Paris to Saint-Rémy-de-Provence and settled into her lovely village at the foot of the Alpilles Mountains.

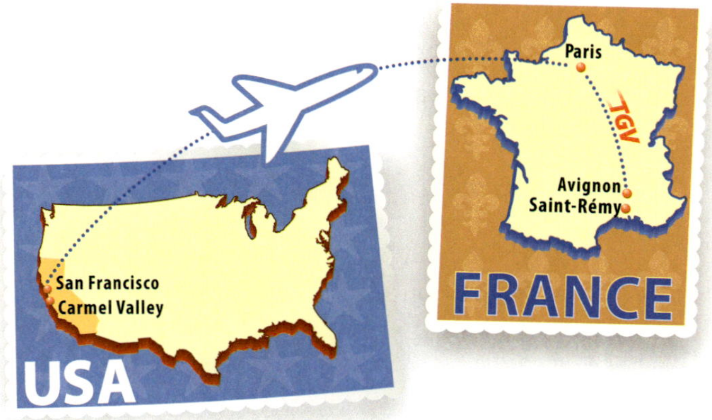

Making her first international flight at nine years of age, Chula proved that an old dog can learn new tricks. She learned to navigate through airports and cross the great divide between *quai* and train. She figured out how to do her business on the hard city streets of Paris. Chula got good at chasing French cats, hiding from wooly sheep, and stealing ripe tomatoes from a *potager,* or French kitchen garden. A true sticky-pawed gourmet.

Two months and many adventures later, Chula headed home. Her last week, she was in one hotel, two countries, and three houses. And she was still smiling.

Here is Chula's story in her own barks.

....1....

A Ticket to Paris

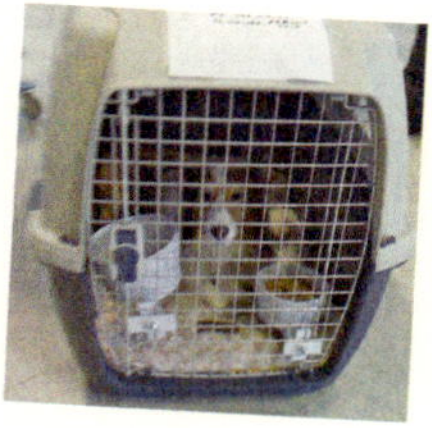

Yes, the trip was *superbe!* But it didn't start out that way. Damn cage. Damn hold. If only I hadn't eaten so many of Bob's good meals, I'd be under 19 pounds and eligible for Business Class. Instead, I spent 11 hours in the hold between a Rottweiler and a Standard Poodle. Didn't dare eat. Couldn't drink. I was sure that I'd never touch ground again.

Once Bob found me, I found my smile! Then it was *un*, *deux*, *trois*, and I was finally free!

Now where's some grass? I had been traveling for 14 hours! When I got out of my cage, there were only shiny floors and concrete. Pardon me, but I just don't go on hard surfaces. We took the elevator up to Floor 5 to get outside. We found busy streets and cars whizzing by, but no patch of grass. Not even a little dirt. We went back down searching for an exit on each floor. No luck.

FINALLY, Bob and Sherry took me on a tram to Roissypôle, the third stop between Charles de Gaulle airport and the TGV station. We went up the escalator (oooh, those things are scary) and out the door to the only grass in town. *Oui! Oui!*

Now, frankly, I thought I deserved a good tummy scratch for making it to the grass. After all, I'm 9 years old x 7 = 63 dog years. You tell me—do you know a 63-year-old human who can hold it that long?

Once we settled into the hotel, I got that tummy scratch from Sherry and some fresh chicken from Bob. He had carried it all the way from California! I drank five cups of water and had to visit the grass at Roissypôle again.

The next day, we rode the TGV down to Saint-Rémy. It was rough getting me and all our luggage on the train, but then I curled up under Bob's legs just like I like. All was fine until the conductor came by and busted me for no ticket! Would he throw me off the speeding train? No, Bob saved the day!

For 5 euros, I got an official ticket. That's when I knew—I'm not just another piece of luggage.

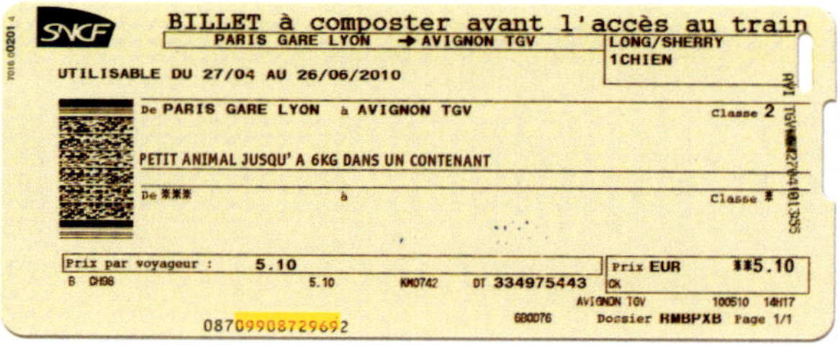
SNCF
BILLET à composter avant l'accès au train
PARIS GARE LYON → AVIGNON TGV
LONG/SHERRY
1CHIEN
UTILISABLE DU 27/04 AU 26/06/2010
De PARIS GARE LYON à AVIGNON TGV Classe 2
PETIT ANIMAL JUSQU'A 6KG DANS UN CONTENANT
De *** à Classe *
Prix par voyageur : 5.10
Prix EUR **5.10
B CH98 5.10 KM0742 DT 334975443
CK
AVIGNON TGV 100510 14H17
08709908729692 680076 Dossier RMBPXB Page 1/1

I also found out why the TGV is called the bullet train—it goes fast, up to 200 miles per hour! About three hours later, we pulled into Avignon, just north of our village, Saint-Rémy-de-Provence. Boy, was I glad to get home and sleep off the jet lag.

2

At Home in Saint-Rémy-de-Provence

I settled in at Avenue de la Libération, one of the spokes off the main road that circles the old part of town. With a street name like that, I was meant to run free!

And I did—I loved my yard! *Oh là là!*

My house was built about 200 years ago next to an old convent.

I had fun digging in the yard and into the history of the house. Over the years a carter, a shoemaker, a tinsmith, and a horse trader lived here. When cars took over from horses, other animals took over the yard. The goats supplied milk and tasty goat cheese. The chickens laid fresh eggs. And the pigs—well, they became pork sausage hung up to dry in what is now the main bathroom. Come to think of it, some of the chickens weren't so lucky either. They ended up as *coq au vin*.

Today, the yard is all mine, except for the CATS! A day or so before I got there, a mother cat had kittens inside the backyard wall. Now it's my job to guard the house, and that requires some measure of barking. Guess that's why the mother cat moved her babies out. One by one, she took them through the gate, up the tree, and over the wall. I was tail-wagging happy! *Au revoir.*

Le Fournil
BOULANGERIE

···· 3 ····

Sniffing Around Provence

Soon I was out and about all over my neighborhood. So many new scents! Right on my street, I caught the sweet smell of baking bread by our neighbors' *boulangerie* and the spicy smell of fresh tomato sauce from the pasta shop next door. I could tell there was a dog two doors down in the real estate office, but it took a lot of sniffing to figure out he was a French bulldog. Of course!

Every time, I walked to town, I stopped at Le Bistro des Alpilles to check out the *plat du jour.* Some days it was bull stew and other days, leg of lamb. Mmm! But when it was salmon, I just walked right on by. Salmon is for cats.

Le Bistrot des Alpilles in Saint-Rémy-de-Provence

I visited other places, too. One day, we all hiked up to an old castle. I never made it to the top. Too many irises to smell along the way.

Every day Sherry goes out for bread, and I go along for the sniff. The bakers are at the heart of a Provençal

village, respected for their centuries-old art. And they know every dog in town.

Sherry's favorite baker is in the Luberon Valley about a half hour from our house. Each trip, I wonder what she'll buy—a *baguette,* of course, but maybe also *les tartes au citron.*

The baker must not make dog biscuits, or I know she'd get me some.

I like it when it takes Sherry a long time to decide on dessert because I get to nose around outside. Did you know the smells by a *pâtisserie* are among the sweetest in Provence?

Not so at the *fromagerie*, or cheese shop. Whew, those smells are strong!

At first, I thought the goat in the window was the culprit, but when I pressed my nose against the glass, I saw that she was plastic. She just stood there being honored for her kin's long history of supplying milk for the tasty *chèvre* made all over Provence.

Banon cheese

Like wine, some cheeses are protected by the *appellation d'origine contrôlée,* or AOC. This designation identifies the region that gives a product its unique quality. The goat cheese *banon,* which comes wrapped in chestnut leaves, bears the AOC of Provence-Alpes-Côtes d'Azur.

Be sure to try it when you're there. It has a unique quality—even though it's all wrapped up, its pungent aroma gets out.

I spent a lot of time at the *fromagerie* trying to sort through the whiffs of *pecorino, gruyère, beaufort, banon,* and many more. I can't tell all these cheeses apart yet, but I certainly know the powerful *banon* when I smell it.

4

Market Days

Every Wednesday in Saint-Rémy is market day—a feast for all my senses. I love the rhythm of the French chatter—people buying and selling, tasting and smelling.

You can shop for everything from veggies, jams, and olive oil to juicy roast chickens to pretty pastel soaps . . .

ARGILE VERTE
HERBES DE PROVENCE
SON
HUILE DE VISON
LAVANDE BROYEE
VANILLE
MIEL

. . . and Provençal tablecloths.

Yes, there's a lot to buy. But me? I go to the market to sniff and taste. On my first visit, I trotted right down to Place Jules-Pellissier, the square in front of the Hôtel de Ville, or City Hall. There, I smelled the fresh garlic even before I saw it.

The vendors piled the garlic high on long tables and chopped it fine to mix with olives in big bowls. What a treat!

I made my way to another pretty table. The spices there made my nose twitch.

Then it was on to the pans of paella. My cheeks began to quiver. I loved it when the paella man dished up his specialty with a friendly *"Voilà"* and dropped a little on the street for me. Sure beats kibble.

I hated to hound the guy at the sausage table, but I wanted to learn the difference between *saucisson à l'âne,* donkey sausage, and *saucisson du taureau,* bull sausage. That donkey stuff tastes, well, just a little different.

All the flowers were sure pretty. I know because they were right at dog's eye level, but really I preferred the sausage table. You can't eat tulips.

People say that every dog has its day, and mine is surely on Wednesday at the Saint-Rémy market.

Here are more markets I like, one for each day of the week.

- **Monday** — Cavaillon
- **Tuesday** — Gordes
- **Wednesday** — Saint-Rémy
- **Thursday** — Aix-en-Provence
- **Friday** — Lourmarin
- **Saturday** — Arles
- **Sunday** — L'Isle-sur-la-Sorgue

5

In Bistros and Cafés

The French have the right respect for dogs—in France we *chiens* get to go to lunch and dinner anytime, anywhere. Bob said, "No barks," and Sherry said, "Under the table." Just a couple of simple rules, and I never got left at home again.

Le Bistrot du Paradou

We enjoyed long, sunny lunches outside. We feasted at soft-light dinners in warm places like Le Bistrot du Paradou.

I loved my close-up view of the bistro's old tile floors.

Better yet were the little bits of crusty bread and cheese that fell on them.

The nutty taste of the Saint-Nectaire was my favorite. It's been made at least since the 1600s, and even Louis XIV had this cheese at his table.

Back home in California, I have safe places that I call "caves"—behind the shoe rack in the closet, under Bob's desk, and in back of the sofa. Peace and quiet—that's what makes a good cave.

In France, the café caves were the best ever! It's a dog's life down there with all the good tastes and no one to bother you. Pretty tablecloths, too.

Sometimes my café caves were so peaceful that I just curled up and went to sleep. *Bonne nuit!*

6
French Traditions

French sidewalk cafes are the very definition of tradition. When you get a good table in a busy sidewalk café, you feel like you're top dog.

In Saint-Rémy, the green tables at the Café des Arts invite you to sit and sip a bit. Sherry and Bob go there for *café au lait* and *croissants* in the morning. I get to come along to catch the falling *croissant* flakes and drink from the water bowl that the café is always kind enough to bring me.

One morning, we met some friends and got a good table right on the street. We followed tradition—*café au lait* and *croissants*. But something was different! People were coming from everywhere and starting to crowd out the view.

I moved to the curb to see what was going on. People stopped to pet me. They thought I was a baby Collie. Not me—I'm a Shetland Sheepdog!

I held my ground at the curb, just waitin' and watchin'. Then my ears perked up. I heard a roll of thunder from down the street. What was it?

3000 SHEEP!

Noisy sheep. Big ole goats.

They just kept coming. Bleating, baa-ing, beh-ing, and clanging their dreadful bells.

It was all too much for me! Yes, I'm a Shetland Sheepdog, but not one who is actively working at the

present time. So I ran for cover. That's my red leash in the picture, and I pulled on it tight from inside my café cave.

Afterward, we all went to an outdoor feast at an old *mas*, or farmhouse. Everyone had lamb, even me!

Over one of those lazy French lunches, I learned why all the sheep were in town.

It was *La Transhumance* when livestock move from the lowlands to the highlands to find more to eat.

It happens every spring during Pentecost in several areas of France. By tradition, shepherds near Saint-Rémy parade their sheep a couple of times around the old village before they head to the highlands.

OK, now I know. And I agree that sheep need to eat, but doggone it! Even for a Shetland Sheepdog, this was all pretty scary.

After lunch, I started to calm down. I followed Bob everywhere. Sherry let me stick close. By the end of the day, I felt much better.

Finally, I was sheepless in Saint-Rémy.

7

Vistas and Villages

A couple of days later, I got my courage up again and went hiking in *Les Alpilles*. As their name implies, these "Little Alps" are small as far as mountains go.

Chalk white limestone juts out from dark green brush growing on the hills. Olive groves and vineyards decorate the valleys. Beautiful views!

View from *Les Alpilles* of the olive groves and vineyards in the Les Baux Valley, Provence.

Up there in *Les Alpilles,* I was outdoors and off-leash just the way I like it! I met a big guy on the trail. Ears back, tail up! I got to show off the white tip on the end of my tail. It's the flag that all Shelties are proud of. Since I live in the USA and France, though, it seems like my white "flag" needs some red and blue, too.

Another day, we drove some curvy roads from Saint-Rémy to Sault.

When we got there, I met St-Marc. *Bonjour!*

St-Marc has watched over Sault since sometime in the 1800s. Standing in front of the *lavoir,* or outdoor washing area, he is known as the protector of washer-women. I wonder if he would protect Sherry when she washes me. I always shake it off and get her all wet!

St-Marc, Sault

St-Marc has a roof with a view! From his high perch in July, he enjoys field upon field of lavender.

You may think it's quiet along the lavender rows, but I hear in dog decibels. The cicadas' song and the bees' buzz hurt my imperfectly tipped Sheltie ears. I had to watch where I poked my nose, too. Those bees can sting!

Still, I padded through the lavender, obeying the Do Not Cut sign. I took nothing but sniffs (and I didn't leave anything either).

When we got to town, there were plenty of beautiful bouquets to buy.

Best of all, I found an extra big water bowl in the square and stopped to take a good drink. Just about every French village has one of these. As I said, the French know how to treat us right.

By this time, I was dog-tired. But when we stopped outside Roussillon, I had to go exploring again.

All along the rolling hills, on both sides of the road, sunflowers were waving in that rich, red soil.

I got up close to take a look. *Uf*—more bees!

As I looked into the sun and stared at those bees, it hit me that the sunflowers were staring back at me. *Eh bien*—that's when I learned that adult sunflowers don't follow the sun. Mostly they just face east.

Our village visits were always busy days. On lazier days, I just meandered. I learned a lot that way, too. I even unearthed the meaning of *Interdit* (Keep Out), but I ignored it and just kept exploring. Most humans don't expect dogs to read.

At this point, I had enjoyed almost two months in Provence. Just when I thought I had seen it all, I ended up in . . . PARIS!

8

Paris Lights and City Sights

In Paris, the City of Light, we stayed on the Left Bank by the Eiffel Tower. Did you know they call the tower the "Iron Lady"? Hmm. Isn't Margaret Thatcher called that, too? Frankly, they don't look anything alike to me. For one thing, Maggie had two legs, and the Parisian Iron Lady has four on the floor, like me.

The Eiffel Tower, completed in 1889, is already over 120 years old. And she's big, too—taller than an 81-story building. Even if I stand on my hind legs, it's hard to take her all in. But I tried—I never got tired of seeing her, day or night.

When the Eiffel Tower opened in 1889 for the Paris World Exposition, it was red. Since then, it's been several other colors, such as yellow, beige, and brick. Now, it's painted "Eiffel Tower brown," but not the same shade all the way up. The painters use three shades of brown, darker at the bottom and paler at the top, for a more pleasing look as the tower pierces the sky. Painting the tower takes 15 months, 25 workers, 60 tons of paint, and 1500 brushes.

After dark, the Iron Lady dresses up in golden lights and then sparkles for ten minutes on the hour. I was bedazzled!

With all her sparkles, the Eiffel Tower seemed to dance and move, but really her four legs stayed in one place. The Carrousel at the base of the tower, though, did go round-and-round while its horses went up and down.

When I took a fun ride, I heard people say, "*Regardez! Regardez!* Look at all those horses and that one lucky dog."

CARROUSEL
de la
TOUR EIFFEL

Just about every day, Bob and I walked along the river Seine, enjoying the views even when we looked down.

View down to the Seine from the Pont Alexandre

Other days, we visited the neighborhoods. We liked to stand on the corner and watch life go by.

CAFE RESTAURANT
CAFE

Of the 37 bridges that cross the Seine in Paris, my favorite is the Pont Alexandre, named after the czar of Russia. With its art nouveau design, it leads in style to the glass-roofed Grand Palais on the Right Bank. Like the Eiffel Tower, the bridge and the Grand Palais were finished in 1889 for the Paris World Exposition.

When you stand in the middle of the Pont Alexandre, the nymphs frame a breathtaking view of Paris.

View of the Seine from the Pont Alexandre

C'est magnifique!

Paris has 20 *arrondissements*, or districts. The Eiffel Tower is in the 7th *arrondissement* on the Left Bank, and the Grand Palais, now the home to special art exhibits and

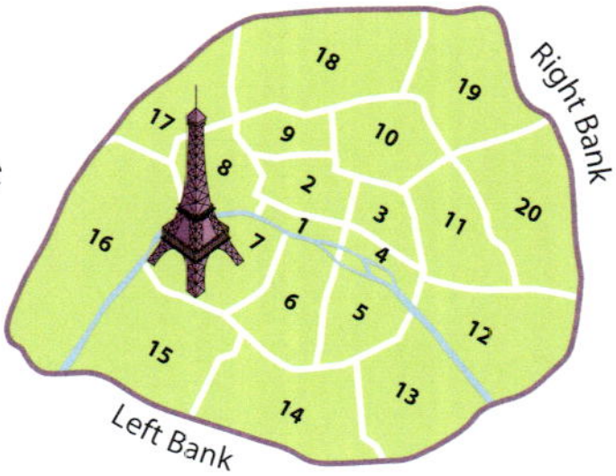

events, is on the Right Bank in the 8th. I explored these *arrondissements* as well as the 3rd and 4th. That's a lot of ground to cover on four little feet! But I kept up, block-by-block and cobblestone-by-cobblestone.

Marais neighborhood near the Saint-Paul Metro

When I looked up, I saw amazing things, like these little gardens growing on the top of a truck in the Marais, one of the oldest neighborhoods in Paris. It's in the 3rd and 4th *arrondissements.*

Along Rue Vielle du Temple in the Marais

When I looked down, I got some helpful hints. It took me two days in Paris to figure out where I was supposed to do my business. Not in the courtyard of the apartment building, that's for sure. I got yelled at there. When Bob took me down the street, though, there was never any grass. Finally, I figured it all out, and this sign really helped.

Paris, however, had other signs I didn't like. Pas de tout!

None of the dogs on those blasted signs looked like a Sheltie. Even so, I wasn't allowed on the Metro. I couldn't play in the parks. I never got into a museum—not one! I was so hoping to smile back at Mona Lisa in the Louvre, but—*c'est la vie*.

On those days when I got left at the apartment, I waited until everyone was gone. Then I hopped up into the big chair and snoozed. (I made sure to leave a lot of fur, too.)

snap!

9

Inside a Paris Gallery

One special night, I did get into a photo show on Île Saint-Louis, an island that sits beautifully in the middle of the Seine. I felt like I was part of history. The first inhabitants of Paris lived on Île de la Cité, the island next-door. In the mid-1600s, Île Saint-Louis was made from a couple of mud banks. Exclusive homes went up along its narrow streets. The fancy homes are still there today, along with cafés, boutiques, galleries, mimes, and an abundance of street life.

Along Rue des Deux Ponts on Île Saint-Louis

Meredith Mullins was exhibiting her work on the theme of *Paris Insolite,* or Unique Paris. By now, I can tell you that Paris is a one-of-a-kind place. *Bien sûr!*

Where else can you see Île Saint-Louis in snow? In one of those rare moments at 5:00 a.m. with

streetlamps aglow, Mullins caught this golden snowstorm in her lens.

Paris wouldn't be Paris without its statues. This guy, though, is having a bad day in the Tuileries Garden. It's hard to imagine not liking the Tuileries, but life is different with a pigeon on your head.

The silhouettes in the sky of Paris are unequaled, especially when a man plays soccer at the top of the world in Montmartre.

Mullins' photographs said *Paris Insolite* in so many different ways. While everyone inside the gallery oohed and aahed over her work, I made a new friend outside on the street.

Then I went to the *soirée* inside, but I was embarrassed about my dirty socks. Too much walking around Paris and too much time under all those tabletops.

When I got back to Saint-Rémy, I visited the *Beauté Canine,* and they cleaned my socks right up. Sparkly white!

10
Au Revoir to France

Mon dieu! No sooner had we gotten back to Saint-Rémy than the day came for us to head home to California.

That morning I scratched out a good spot, turned around three times, and plopped down in the shade of the old olive tree in my backyard.

Then I made the rounds in Saint-Rémy one lovely last time.

I trotted past the old stone auge,

out my gate,

down the street by
the neighbor's boulangerie,

and right up to the Trinity fountain,

where I got my
nose wet!

Then I took off down
old Rue Carnot,

a-zigging
and a-zagging,

past the boucherie, or
butcher shop, to the other
side of the street.

One stop at the salt shop—
quick sniff,

and I was on to the fountain of Nostradamus, who was born in Saint-Rémy in 1503.

Nostradamus was an apothecary and an astrologer, but he is most famous for his prophecies written in French quatrains.

Dog Leg Left,
I took Rue Carnot

to beautiful Place Favier,

where I walked on
its well-worn stones.

Homes dating from the 15th century look out on Place Favier. One houses the Musée des Alpilles.

Then it was back into town
to hear some jazz,

and I got to sing along!

Next I trotted up the steps to the Hôtel de Ville

Hôtel de Ville, or City Hall

to admire the French national motto:
Liberté, Egalité, Fraternité.

Then I stopped at a shop on the square,

went past the big church,

Collégiale Saint-Martin,
rebuilt around 1820,
maintains its 14th Century spire.

and arrived at Place de la République,
where something's always going on!

This busy square replaced the medieval ramparts.

Oh, no! Time to head home?

I made my way past bistros

and bars.

Then I stopped to say
hi to a friend going by

and came to the end of my walk.
I took a L-o-o-ng last look at Saint-Rémy.

Back at my door,
I thought to myself:

"Lucky me!
What a lovely walk
in Saint-Rémy."

When we packed up and left town, we drove through tunnels of plane trees. The majestic plane trees are a signature of Saint-Rémy. They line the roads going in and out of town. Some say Napoleon planted the trees across

Provence to provide shade for his troops as they marched through France. I don't know if that's true, but I do know this: When you're looking for shade on a hot day in Provence, try barking up a plane tree.

We made it to Avignon in time to catch the TGV to Paris, and this time I had my ticket. We spent the night at Paris CDG, and then I was back in that damn cage and on my way home. (I finally did figure out how to take a drink.)

It was a long trip home! Eighteen hours later, I was on Highway 101 heading south from San Francisco. I got to sit up front and navigate. After all, I'm a dog who has trotted the globe.

Finally, I was home. Ah, it felt good to sniff the Carmel Valley air again.

I like it here in California. So I'll stay for now, chase squirrels, try to avoid the skunks in the way backyard, and dream of Paris and Provence.

But when spring comes around, I plan to trot the globe again. Maybe I'll go back to France or enjoy the pepperoni pizza at the port in Naples. I could howl with the howler monkeys in Mexico or stand nose-to-nose with the Great Sphinx of Giza. Who knows where I'll travel next, but one thing's for sure—

You can't keep a good dog home
once she's seen "Parie"!

···· Afterword ····

How to Take Your Pup to France

You'll need a few papers, an airline-approved crate, and ***a sense of humor***.

Most airlines allow dogs inside the cabin only if they fit in a carrier small enough to go under the seat. That's why Chula, a 30-pound Sheltie, had to travel in the hold, where there is a pressurized, heated compartment for animals. You'll need to reserve a space and pay for your pet's ticket. Chula's ticket was about $100 each way, though rates vary with airlines and destinations.

Non-stop flights are best. If you have to change planes, quiz the airline on how they transfer pets. Some even have pet hotels and air-conditioned waiting vans to avoid too much time on the tarmac. The dates you choose to travel matter since airlines will not transport pets in very hot or very cold weather.

The crate type and size are also important. We found the right type of crate for Chula by checking web sites on pet travel.

Measure your dog to help you choose the right size. How long should the crate be? While your dog stands, measure its length from the base of its tail to the tip of its nose, and then add 4 inches. How wide should the crate be? Measure from the floor to the top of your dog's head, and then add 4 inches. Your dog should be able to turn around and to stand upright without bending its head.

On top of the crate, affix a large sticker with your pet's name, airline and flight number, departure and destination cities with the planned departure and arrival times, and phone numbers to call. Aside from this sticker, airlines do not permit anything on the outside of the carrier.

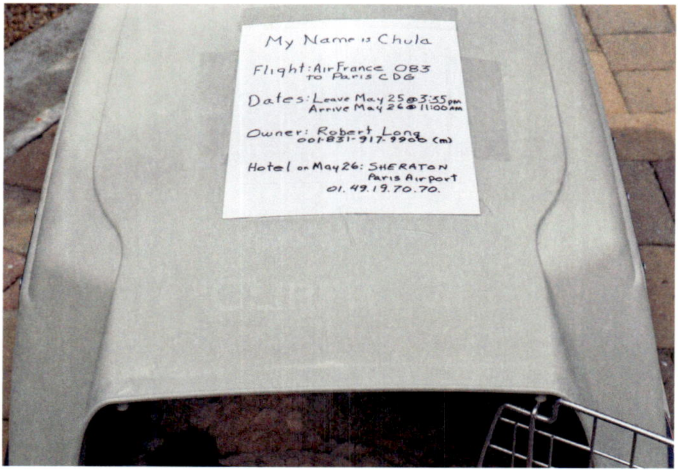

Once a pet is on board, no one can check on it. So, be sure to outfit the crate with a supply of food and water, a comfy pad, and your pet's favorite toy or something that carries your scent.

Dehydration during the flight is the greatest danger. Get your vet's advice, of course, but most experts in the pet transport field do not recommend sedatives since they can increase the risk of dehydration.

Take special care that your dog has water. Open food and water bowls bolt onto the crate like this:

However, water can easily spill out during boarding and bumpy rides. You can freeze the water up until boarding as one precaution.

A product called Waterbites, offers a hydrating gel that can't spill out. A drip bottle fastened to the inside of the crate works well if you have taught your dog how to lick the ball at the end of the tube to get the water. A little peanut butter on the end of the tube speeds the learning process!

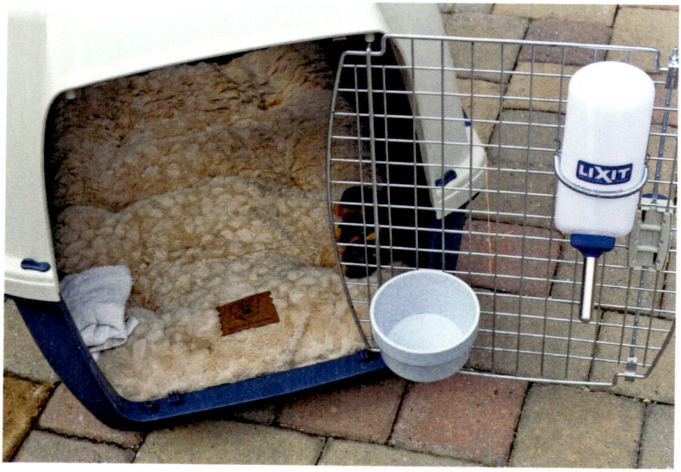

To enter France, your dog must have a microchip. This subcutaneous chip, implanted by your vet, contains a scannable identification number. A US microchip will not register on all types of scanning equipment used in France, so you may want to carry a portable scanner that can prove your dog has a microchip.

And now for the sense of humor part . . .

Every country has its bureaucracy, and you'll have to cut some red tape to get your pet's passport. Visit **OIC-Books.com** for samples and sources of all forms.

To travel between France and the USA, your pet will need:

- **EU Health Certificate (Form EU 998)** You can buy this form online. Your vet has to complete the form to prove that, during the last 12 months, your dog has had all the necessary vaccinations (for France: distemper, hepatitis, parvo, leptospirosis, DHLPP, and rabies).

  The vet also records the pet's identification number from the microchip. Rules are rules. So know that this form is one sheet, front and back, and cannot be submitted as two separate sheets.

- **USDA Endorsement** Next you must send the completed form along with the microchip implant record and the rabies certificate to the US Department of Agriculture for certification that your vet is properly licensed and the information is complete, accurate, and timely. The USDA will stamp the form and send it back to you. Enclose payment for this service, $35 in 2010.

This all takes time, so start early but not too early—the EU Health Certificate and its endorsement must be dated no more than four months before departure.

- **International Health Certificate** Your vet should have this form. It certifies that your pet is healthy enough for air travel and must be completed within ten days of departure.

We had some frustrations getting all the paperwork together and hope these notes ease the process for you. It's important to check regulations for the specific country you plan to visit and the specific airline you plan to take. For example, France and the US have no quarantine period, but other countries, such as England, do. Visit **OIC-Books.com** for links to organizations with up-to-date information on regulations.

Despite the paperwork challenges, the trip with Chula was pure pleasure. And in our case, not one immigration or customs official asked for the papers, although in Paris the Air France check-in agent did review Chula's International Health Certificate.

One last thing—pets always arrive in a special area of baggage claim. Expect to wait a while for your pup, and expect to see a real big tail wag as soon as your pup sees you!

Bon voyage!

Sherry, Robert, and Chula Wula D'Augue

Acknowledgments and Credits

Chula Wula D'Augue wishes to thank the following individuals, whose contributions enriched this book and helped to make it a *fait accompli*:

Marcia Bateman, Andrea Carter, Julie Cason, Darius Detwiler, Brigitte Echaiti, Mohamed Echaiti, Gaston Georis, Jeanne Gesumaria, Samuel Gesumaria, Jeri Gibson, Ray Godfrey, Kathleen Kraft, Charles Meagher, Meredith Mullins, Erick Paraiso, John Pichel, William Roden, and Carol Starr.

Vive la belle France! Vivent les bons chiens!

Design & Illustration

Creative Direction: Jeri Gibson
Cover Design and Illustration: Darius Detwiler
Map Design and Illustration (Foreword and Chapters 4, 7, and 8): Mapping Specialists and Darius Detwiler
OIC logo: Charles Meagher
OIC face: Charles Meagher and Darius Detwiler

Illustrations

Cover and all interior page illustrations: Darius Detwiler.

Photographs

Cover and Flaps

Eiffel Tower: © Erick Paraiso; illumination of Eiffel Tower © Tour Eiffel-Illuminations Pierre Bideau. Sunflowers: © graphixel / iStockphoto. Lights on Pont Alexandre: © Robert Long. Spices: © Jean Gill / iStockphoto. Sherry and Chula: © Robert Long. Bob and Chula: © Sheron Long.

Title Page

Chula at Fountain in Sault: © Robert Long. Rose petals: © Dawn Poland / iStockphoto.

Contents

Melons in a crate: © Robert Paul van Beets / iStockphoto. Eiffel Tower © Sheron Long.

Foreword: A Sheltie Goes to France!

7 Chula smiling: © Robert Long.

Chapter 1: A Ticket to Paris

9 Chula in cage: © Sheron Long. 10-11 Bob and Chula; Chula coming out of cage: © Sheron Long. Chula in grass: © Erick Paraiso. 12-13 Bob and Chula at train; Chula asleep: © Sheron Long. TGV: © Alain & Josyane Cassigne / Photolibrary.

Chapter 2: At Home in Saint-Rémy-de-Provence

15 La Liberation sign: © Sheron Long. 16-17 Chula in yard: © Robert Long. 18-19 House: © Jeri Gibson. Cat going out of gate; Cat going up tree: © Robert Long.

Chapter 3: Sniffing Around Provence

21 Chula sniffing by wall: © Sheron Long. 22-23 Le Bistro des Alpilles: © Robert Long. Chula in irises: © Sheron Long. 24-25 Dog by bakery: © Owen Franken / Corbis Images. 26-27 French pastries: © Lillis Photography / iStockphoto. Chula at cheese shop: © Robert Long. 28-29 Banon cheese: © Bon Appetit / Alamy. Collection of cheeses: © Nikolay Stefanov Dimitrov / Shutterstock.

Chapter 4: Market Days

31 Tomatoes in crate: © PCL / Alamy. 32-33 Saint-Rémy market scene: © Sheron Long. Lavender bouquets: © Mytho / iStockphoto. Provençal dresses; Strawberries in baskets: © Jean Gill / iStockphoto. Olive plants: © astrada / iStockphoto. 34-35 Vegetables on tables and cart: © Purestock / Getty Images. Roasting chickens: © Evgeniya Uvarova / Shutterstock. Soaps: © Josep Lluis Grau / Shutterstock. 36-37 Textiles: © INSADCO Photography / Alamy. Fresh garlic: © Dr. Heinz Linke / iStockphoto. 38-39 Olives: © Robert Long. Spices: © Jean Gill / iStockphoto. 40-41 Pans of paella: © Sheron Long. Sausage: © Nikolay Stefanov Dimitrov / Shutterstock. 42 Flowers: © Dan Moore / iStockphoto.

Chapter 5: In Bistros and Cafés

45 Bistro chair: © Sheron Long. 46-47 Le Bistro du Paradou: © Robert Long. Lunch outside; Plates with eggplant and foie gras: © Sheron Long. 48-49 Chula on tile floor; Cheese plate: © Sheron Long. 50-51 Chula under table; Chula asleep in café: © Sheron Long.

Chapter 6: French Traditions

53 Croissants in basket: © Flariviere / Shutterstock. 54-55 Friend

and Chula in café; Chula at curb (3 pictures): © Sheron Long. 56-57 Sheep in the street: © Robert Long. 58-59 Close-up of sheep: © Robert Long. 60-61 Sheep with Chula's leash: © Robert Long. 62-63 Chula by roasted lamb; Couple at table: © Sheron Long. 64-65 *La Transhumance* poster; Chula following Bob; Chula at Sherry's feet: © Sheron Long.

Chapter 7: Vistas and Villages
67 Tower: © Robert Long. 68-69 View of Les Alpilles valley: © Art Kowalsky / Alamy. Chula and white dog: © Erick Paraiso. 70-71 Sault, France: © Steve Vidler / Photolibrary. St-Marc: © Sheron Long. 72-73 Lavender field: © Carol Starr. 74-75 Lavender field with building: © Photodisc / Photolibrary. "Do not cut the lavender" sign: © Sheron Long. 76-77 Lavender on sale in Sault: © Sheron Long. Chula at Fountain in Sault: © Robert Long. 78-79 Sunflower panorama: © Carol Starr. 80-81 Sunflower with bees: © Sheron Long. Interdit sign: © Robert Long.

Chapter 8: Paris Lights and City Sights
83 Lights on Pont Alexandre: © Robert Long. 84-85 Eiffel Tower during the day: © Erick Paraiso. 86-87 Eiffel Tower at night: © Erick Paraiso; illumination of Eiffel Tower © Tour Eiffel-Illuminations Pierre Bideau. 89 Eiffel Tower and Carrousel: © Erick Paraiso; illumination of Eiffel Tower © Tour Eiffel-Illuminations Pierre Bideau. "Tour Eiffel" is a trademark of the Société d'Exploitation de la Tour Eiffel. 90-91 Bird over Seine; Bob and Chula on street corner: © Sheron Long. 92-93 Panorama from Pont Alexandre: © Lena Stutz / Alamy. 94-95 Nymph framing view from Pont Alexandre: © Sheron Long. 96-97 Chula walking in the Marais: © Erick Paraiso. 98-99 Garden baskets on car in Marais; Dog and arrow on pavement: © Sheron Long. 100-101 cobblestone street (background) © Alvaro Arroyo / iStockphoto. "No Dogs" signs 1 and 4: © Robert Long. "No Dogs" signs 2 and 3: © Meredith Mullins. 102 Children at museum: © DiMaggio/Kalish / Photolibrary. 103 Chula asleep in chair: © Erick Paraiso.

Chapter 9: Inside a Paris Gallery
105 Gallery sign: © Sheron Long. 106-107 Bob and Chula in front of gallery; Photograph in frame: © Sheron Long. Photograph in

gallery window by Bob and Chula: *Les Jardins de Luxembourg* © Meredith Mullins. Gallery posters through window: © Sheron Long. Photograph on book cover in gallery window: *Le Parapluie* © Meredith Mullins; Photograph on *Paris Insolite* Exhibition Invitation in gallery window: *Tango* © Meredith Mullins. 108-109 View of Île Saint-Louis in the snow: *La Neige* (Île St-Louis at 5 am) © Meredith Mullins. This photograph won the *Grand Concours Photo sur Paris* in 2009. 110-111 Statue with bird: *Les Amis des Tuileries* © Meredith Mullins. Man kicking soccer ball: *Montmartre*: © Meredith Mullins. See more photography by Meredith Mullins at www.meredithmullins.com 112-113 Chula and dog on sidewalk (3 pictures): © Sheron Long. 114-115 Chula with dirty paws in gallery; Chula with clean paws by fountain: © Sheron Long.

Chapter 10: Au Revoir to France
117 Urn with flowers: © Sheron Long. 118-119 Chula under olive tree; Stone *auge* with flowers: © Sheron Long. Out my gate: © Carol Starr. 120-121 Buildings along street; Trinity fountain (2 photos): © Robert Long. 122-123 Rue Carnot (3 photos): © Robert Long. 124-125 Salt Shop: © Robert Long; Nostradamus fountain: © Robert Long. Nostradamus fountain (detail): © Erick Paraiso. 126-127 View down Rue Carnot: © Robert Long. Place Favier; Stone tiles: © Sheron Long. 128-129 Jazz musicians: © Robert Long. Chula singing: © Sheron Long. 130-131 Hôtel de Ville (2 photos): © Robert Long. 132-133 Storefront: © Sheron Long. Church: © Erick Pariso. 134-135 Place de la République (2 photos): © Robert Long. 136-137 Sad Chula: © Jeanne Gesumaria. Bistro; Bar: © Robert Long. Dog on Street: © Erick Paraiso. 138-139 View of Saint-Rémy: © Robert Long. 140-141 Chula in doorway: © Erick Paraiso. Chula on leash: © Robert Long. 142-143 Plane trees lining the road: © Travelpix Ltd / Getty Images. 145 Chula and Bob in car: © Erick Paraiso. 146-147 Carmel Valley sign; Chula sniffing: © Robert Long. Bob, Sherry, and Chula in front of Eiffel Tower: © Erick Paraiso; illumination of Eiffel Tower © Tour Eiffel-Illuminations Pierre Bideau.

Afterword: How to Take Your Pup to France
All photos: © Robert Long

The End

OIC-Books.com

Visit our site for more on Shelties, dogs, pet travel, and France.